To Alyssa, William, and Olive
—J.J.

For Allison
—P.O.

The Good Egg
Text copyright © 2019 Jory John
Illustrations copyright © 2019 by Pete Oswald
All rights reserved. Printed in the United States of America.
No part of this book may be used or reproduced in any manner whatsoever
without written permission except in the case of brief quotations embodied
in critical articles and reviews. For information address
HarperCollins Children's Books, a division of HarperCollins Publishers,
195 Broadway, New York, NY 10007.
www.harpercollinschildrens.com

ISBN 978-0-06-286600-4

The artist used scanned watercolor textures
and digital paint to create the illustrations for this book.
Typography by Jeanne Hogle
18  19  20  21  PC  10  9  8  7  6  5  4  3  2
❖
First Edition

# THE GOOD EGG

milk

ueberry

One Dozen

Fresh Eggs

From the creators of *The Bad Seed*

Jory John and Pete Oswald

**HARPER**
*An Imprint of HarperCollinsPublishers*

Oh, hello!
I was just rescuing this cat.
Know why?
Because I'm a good egg.

A *verrrrrry* good egg.

It's true.
I do all kinds of good things. Like . . .

. . . I'll carry your groceries.

I'll water your plants.

I'll change your tires.

I'll paint your house.

If you need any help whatsoever, I'm your egg.

I've *always* been a good egg. It's been this way from the start. Even in my earliest days . . .

. . . back at the store.

There were a dozen of us, living together under one recycled roof.

There was Meg. And Peg. And Greg. And Clegg. And Shel. And Shelly. And Sheldon. And Shelby. And Egbert. And Frank. And *other* Frank.

The other eleven eggs weren't on their best behavior.
They weren't exactly . . . good.

They ignored
their bedtime.

They only ate
sugary cereal.

**They threw tantrums.**

**They cried for no reason.**

**They broke their stuff . . . *on purpose!***

Meanwhile, I tried to take charge.
I tried to fix their bad behavior.
I tried to keep the peace.
Because I was a good egg.

A *verrrrrry* good egg.

Nobody seemed to care, though.

Sigh

Every night, I was exhausted.
My head felt scrambled.

Then, one fateful morning, I noticed some cracks in my shell.

They were *everywhere.*

My doctor said it was from all the pressure
I was putting on myself. The pressure of
making sure everybody was as good as me.

I was cracking up . . . *literally!*
Something *had* to change.
**I'd had enough!**

I told Meg and Peg and Greg and Clegg and Shel and Shelly and Sheldon and Shelby and Egbert and Frank and *other* Frank that I was leaving.

"I can't be the only good egg in a bad carton," I said.
"Blah blah blah," they replied.

I left that night.

I wandered from town to town.

The hours became days.

The days became weeks.

I lost track of time.

I was alone.

Out there, on the road, under the stars, I really tried to focus on myself and what *I* needed.

I took walks.

I read books.

I floated in the river.

I wrote in my journal.

I found simple moments to be quiet.

I breathed in.

I breathed out.

I even started painting.

**For once, I found time for *me*.**

# And guess what!

Little by little, the cracks in my shell started to heal.
My head no longer felt scrambled.

I started to feel like myself again.

So I've made a big decision.
I'm returning to my old carton and my friends.
Besides, I'm kind of lonely out here.

**This time, I know what I need to do.**

I'll try not to worry so much.

I'll be good to my fellow eggs while also being good to *myself*.

"Here we go. . . ."

Everybody missed me. I missed them, too.

"Hello, Meg. Howdy, Peg. Hey, Greg. Greetings, Clegg. What's up, Shel? Aloha, Shelly. Hey-o, Sheldon. Hi, Shelby. Good day, Egbert. What's happening, Frank? Howdy do, *other* Frank?"

Sure, every once in a while,
somebody's still a little bit bad.

But it's not like before.

Here's what I realized:
The other eggs aren't perfect,
and I don't have to be, either.

I'm OK with that.

Yep, the ol' carton is back together!
We're a solid dozen again.

It's good to be home.